THE CREATION

James Weldon Johnson

illustrated by

James E. Ransome

Holiday House / New York

To African-American artists who have succeeded with dignity and pride:

Romare Bearden

William H. Johnson

Tom Feelings

Ernest Crichlow

Jerry Pinkney

Henry O. Tanner

Jacob Lawrence

E. Simms Campbell

Robert Freeman

to name only a few . . . all who have touched my life.

JAMES E. RANSOME

Illustrations copyright © 1994 by James E. Ransome
ALL RIGHTS RESERVED
Printed in the United States of America

Library of Congress Cataloging-in-Publication Data
The Creation / by James Weldon Johnson ; illustrated by James Ransome.
— 1st ed.
p.   cm.
Summary: A poem based on the story of creation from the first book
of the Bible.
ISBN 0-8234-1069-2
1. Creation—Juvenile poetry.   2. Children's poetry, American.
[1. Creation—Poetry.   2. American poetry—Afro-American authors.
3. Bible stories—O.T.]   I. Ransome, James.   II. Johnson, James
Weldon, 1871–1938. Creation.
PS3519.O2625C73   1994   93–3207   CIP   AC
811'.52—dc20
ISBN 0-8234-1207-5 (pbk.)

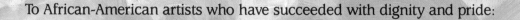

Illustrator's Note

James Weldon Johnson's poetic sermons in *God's Trombones: Seven Negro Sermons in Verse* were influenced by the folk sayings and southern imagery of nineteenth-century African-American plantation preachers. I have tried to remain faithful to the spirit of Mr. Johnson's text by interspersing creation scenes with images of a southern country storyteller.

James E. Ransome
January 15, 1993

And God stepped out on space,—
And he looked around and said,
"I'm lonely—
I'll make me a world."

And far as the eye of God could see
Darkness covered everything,
Blacker than a hundred midnights
Down in a cypress swamp.

Then God smiled,
And the light broke,
And the darkness rolled up on one side,
And the light stood shining on the other,
And God said, *"That's good!"*

Then God reached out and took the light in His hands,
And God rolled the light around in His hands
Until He made the sun;
And He set that sun a-blazing in the heavens.
And the light that was left from making the sun
God gathered up in a shining ball
And flung against the darkness,
Spangling the night with the moon and stars.
Then down between
The darkness and the light
He hurled the world;
And God said, *"That's good!"*

Then God himself stepped down—
And the sun was on His right hand,
And the moon was on His left;
The stars were clustered about His head,
And the earth was under His feet.
And God walked, and where He trod
His footsteps hollowed the valleys out
And bulged the mountains up.

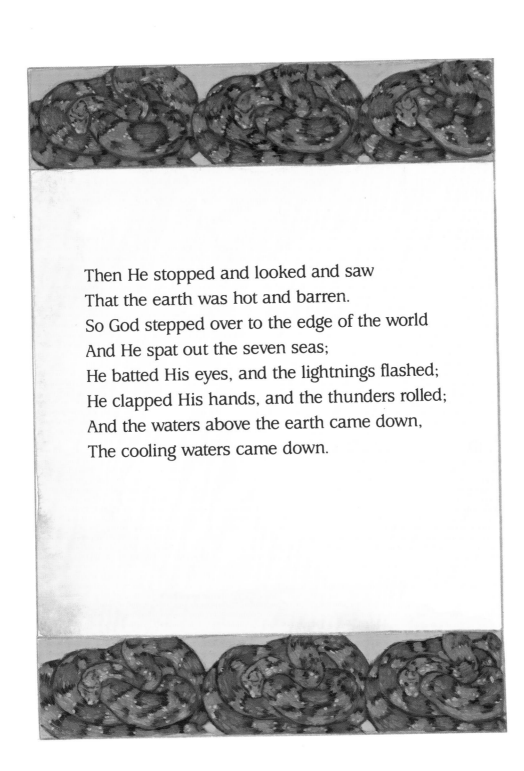

Then He stopped and looked and saw
That the earth was hot and barren.
So God stepped over to the edge of the world
And He spat out the seven seas;
He batted His eyes, and the lightnings flashed;
He clapped His hands, and the thunders rolled;
And the waters above the earth came down,
The cooling waters came down.

Then the green grass sprouted,
And the little red flowers blossomed,
The pine-tree pointed his finger to the sky,
And the oak spread out his arms;
The lakes cuddled down in the hollows of the ground,
And the rivers ran down to the sea;
And God smiled again,
And the rainbow appeared,
And curled itself around His shoulder.

Then God raised His arm and He waved his hand
Over the sea and over the land,
And He said, *"Bring forth! Bring forth!"*
And quicker than God could drop His hand,
Fishes and fowls
And beasts and birds
Swam the rivers and the seas,
Roamed the forests and the woods,
And split the air with their wings,
And God said, *"That's good!"*

Then God walked around,
And God looked around
On all that He had made.
He looked at His sun,
And He looked at His moon,
And He looked at His little stars;
He looked on His world
With all its living things,
And God said, *"I'm lonely still."*

Then God sat down
On the side of a hill where He could think;
By a deep, wide river He sat down;
With His head in His hands,
God thought and thought,
Till He thought, *"I'll make me a man!"*

Up from the bed of the river
God scooped the clay;
And by the bank of the river
He kneeled Him down;
And there the great God Almighty
Who lit the sun and fixed it in the sky,
Who flung the stars to the most far corner of the night,
Who rounded the earth in the middle of His hand—
This Great God,
Like a mammy bending over her baby,
Kneeled down in the dust
Toiling over a lump of clay
Till He shaped it in His own image;

Then into it He blew the breath of life,
And man became a living soul.

Amen. Amen.